A lucky shot?

Mia unhooked her bra

pocket on th

basketball c

it and sudde

penny.

Mia quickly rubbed the charm between her fingers.

"You're in," the coach yelled, pushing Mia toward the court.

With only fifteen seconds left, Juan snatched the rebound and dribbled down the court.

"Over here!" Mia shouted.

Juan hurled the ball toward her.

Mia spun toward the basket and bounced off her feet. She released the ball in midair. It jiggled around the rim of the basket and dropped in as the game clock buzzed.

The final score flashed on the scoreboard. Titans 38. Wolverines 37.

To my mother and my husband, who both made
writing this book possible, and to Christopher
for your creative inspiration.
—C. K. R.

PUFFIN BOOKS
Published by the Penguin Group
Penguin Young Readers Group,
345 Hudson Street, New York, New York 10014, U.S.A.
Penguin Group (Canada), 10 Alcorn Avenue, Toronto, Ontario,
Canada M4V 3B2 (a division of Pearson Penguin Canada Inc.)
Penguin Books Ltd, 80 Strand, London WC2R 0RL, England
Penguin Ireland, 25 St Stephen's Green, Dublin 2, Ireland
(a division of Penguin Books Ltd)
Penguin Group (Australia), 250 Camberwell Road, Camberwell,
Victoria 3124, Australia (a division of Pearson Australia Group Pty Ltd)
Penguin Books India Pvt Ltd, 11 Community Centre,
Panchsheel Park, New Delhi - 110 017, India
Penguin Group (NZ), Cnr Airborne and Rosedale Roads, Albany,
Auckland 1310, New Zealand (a division of Pearson New Zealand Ltd)
Penguin Books (South Africa) (Pty) Ltd, 24 Sturdee Avenue,
Rosebank, Johannesburg 2196, South Africa

Registered Offices: Penguin Books Ltd, 80 Strand, London WC2R 0RL, England

First published in the United States of America by Dial Books for Young Readers
and Puffin Books, divisions of Penguin Young Readers Group, 2005

1   3   5   7   9   10   8   6   4   2

LIBRARY OF CONGRESS CATALOGING-IN-PUBLICATION DATA

Richardson, Charisse K.
The real lucky charm / Charisse K. Richardson; illustrated by Eric Velasquez.
p. cm.
Summary: Thinking that luck—rather than hard work—has helped her succeed
on the court and at school, ten-year-old Mia panics and turns to her twin brother
for help when her lucky gold basketball goes missing from her charm bracelet.
ISBN 0-14-240431-4 (paperback)—ISBN 0-8037-3105-1
[1. Superstition—Fiction. 2. Luck—Fiction. 3. Charm bracelets—Fiction.
4. Basketball—Fiction. 5. Twins—Fiction. 6. Brothers and sisters—Fiction.
7. Schools—Fiction.] I. Velasquez, Eric, ill. II. Title.
PZ7.R39432Rc 2005 [Fic]—dc22 2005047584

Manufactured in China

THE REAL LUCKY CHARM

by Charisse K. Richardson

illustrated by Eric Velasquez

PUFFIN BOOKS

CHAPTER 1

"**L**ook at all the stuff there is to do," Mia Robinson said, stepping out of the boys' basketball line on Saturday afternoon. She read the signs on the tables in the gym. "Art. Drama. Football. Ballet."

"I didn't know they had so many choices," Gabbie Gilbert, Mia's best friend, said.

"Me either," Mia said. It was her first time attending Fall Sign-up Day at the recreation center. She came with Marcus, her twin brother, who was standing in the boys' basketball line. Mia and Gabbie had come along because their mom promised to take them to the movies afterward.

Mia glanced over at the next registration table. She hadn't noticed the table earlier. But now the sign on it caught her attention:

WANTED: A FEW GOOD GIRLS!

A tall woman standing behind the table waved at the girls. "Looking for something fun to do?" she called out.

"Sort of," Mia said in a curious voice. She noticed a second sign on the table that said: GIRLS BASKETBALL.

"I'll be right back," Mia said.

"Wait for me!" Gabbie said, following Mia to the girls' basketball table.

"Hi," the lady said, "I'm Coach Dilbert."

Mia and Gabbie introduced themselves.

"I didn't know we could sign up for *girls'* basketball," Mia said.

"This is the first year," Coach Dilbert said. "Would you girls like to join a team?"

"Sure!" Mia blurted. "I'll ask my mom when she finishes registering my brother."

Gabbie gave Mia a puzzled look. "I thought

you weren't going to sign up for anything."

"I wasn't," Mia said. "But that was *before* I knew they had a girls' basketball team." Like lots of ten-year-olds, playing basketball was one of Mia's favorite things. She enjoyed it almost as much as writing and bike riding.

Coach Dilbert smiled at Gabbie. "We can find a spot for you, too," she said.

Gabbie hunched her shoulders. "I've never played on a basketball team before."

"Neither have I," Mia said. "Come on! It will be lots of fun."

Gabbie swayed from side to side. "All right, I'll join," she said.

"I'm done!" Marcus said, walking over to Mia. "We can go to the movies now."

"Not yet," Mia told her brother. "I want to sign up for basketball, too."

"Huh?" Marcus said.

Mia pointed to the sign on the table. "The *girls'* basketball team."

"That's great, honey!" their mom said, join-

ing them. "I'm glad you found an activity."

"Cool!" Marcus said. He was still psyched from his last basketball season. He was MVP of the Titans, his recreation center team.

"I want to play, too," Gabbie told Mrs. Robinson.

"We'll get a registration form to take home to your parents," Mrs. Robinson said.

When they got back in the minivan, Mia called her dad from her mom's cell phone. "Guess what, Dad?!" Mia said. "I joined a basketball team."

"A *girls'* basketball team," Marcus added.

•   •   •

It was a few hours later when they got home from the movies. The phone was ringing when they walked into the house.

"I'll get it," Mia said, dashing into the kitchen. She grabbed the phone off the kitchen counter and pressed it against her ear.

"Oh, hi Coach Dilbert," she said. Mia

hadn't expected to hear from her new basketball coach so soon.

"Really?!" Mia asked. She sounded surprised. "Okay. Yes, I'll tell them."

Mia hung up the phone and whirled around. She had a glow in her eyes like a reporter who just got a juicy news scoop. "They aren't having a girls' team after all," Mia said. "Not enough girls signed up."

"So what do we do now?" Gabbie asked.

"The coaches are combining the eight-to-ten-year-old girls' and boys' teams," Mia said. "There's only going to be one team for kids our age. A co-ed team!"

Marcus coughed and almost choked on a piece of candy. "You mean the girls are going to play on the *boys'* team?" Marcus asked.

"The *co-ed* team," Mia said, correcting him.

"Are you serious?" Marcus asked. "Who are we going to play?"

"All-boys teams," Mia said. "We'll be the first and only co-ed team in our league."

"I don't believe this," Marcus said. "I wonder if Juan knows yet." He picked up the phone and went to call his best friend.

Mia grabbed two sports drinks from the refrigerator. "The co-ed team will make a great story for my newspaper," Mia said. She was always thinking about ideas for *Mia's World*. She started the newspaper after her class took a tour of the local newspaper plant. After that field trip, Mia was sure of two things: she wanted to be a reporter, and she was going to start her very own newspaper.

Mia tossed Gabbie one of the drinks. "This is big news!" Mia said.

Gabbie's head drooped. "I can't play on the same team as Marcus and Juan," she said.

"Why not?" Mia asked.

"I'm not good enough," Gabbie said.

"But you'll be playing *with* them. Not against them," Mia said.

Gabbie sipped her drink. "It's different for you," she said. "You're used to playing with

Marcus. You practice with him all the time."

"But you won't be alone," Mia said. "I'll be on the team. And there will be other girls on the team, too. I'll help you. I promise."

Gabbie lifted her head. "Promise?" she asked.

Mia took her finger and drew a circle around her heart. Then she made a fist and lightly tapped her heart two times. "Promise!" Mia said. "Best friends' honor."

"Okay, then. I'll play," Gabbie said. She drew a circle around her heart, and tapped it twice with her fist. "Best friends' honor."

CHAPTER 2

On Monday afternoon, the twins' dad walked into the house from work carrying a shopping bag. "I'm home!" he shouted.

"You're home early," Mrs. Robinson yelled from the family room. She was sitting in front of the computer pecking away at the keyboard.

"Hi, Dad," Mia said, dashing down the steps. She followed her dad into the family room. "Are you taking us to basketball practice?"

He smiled as he placed the shopping bag on the coffee table. "It's your first one," he said. "I wouldn't miss it."

Just then, Marcus walked into the room. "Hi, Dad," he said. "What's in the bag?"

Mr. Robinson pulled out a tiny gift box and gave it to Mia. "A little something for the newest basketball player in our family," he said.

Mia ripped the wrapping paper off the box and opened it. Her eyes twinkled as she saw a shiny gold charm under the tissue paper. It was a miniature basketball. "Another charm for my bracelet!" she said. Mia already had a cross, a writer's scroll, a heart, and the letter *M* charm on her bracelet.

Mia stood on her tiptoes and gave her dad a tight hug. "Thanks, Dad!"

Mr. Robinson reached back into the bag. "And this is for you," he said, handing a box to Marcus.

Marcus grinned. "This is awesome!" he said, pulling a Jason Carter jersey from the box. Jason Carter was his favorite professional basketball player. "Thanks a million, Dad!"

"You're welcome," Mr. Robinson said. "I knew you really missed your old jersey."

"I sure did," Marcus said. His old Jason

Carter jersey had been his favorite. But it had shrunk in the dryer months ago—the same day that Marcus and Mia's class had met Jason Carter at Giants Practice Day. Marcus had been saving for a new one ever since then.

Mia handed the new basketball charm to her dad. "Can you please put this on?" she asked.

Mr. Robinson slid the charm on Mia's bracelet and rubbed it between two fingers. "This charm reminds me of the lucky penny I had in high school," he said. "I used to rub it before all of my basketball games."

"You did?" Mia asked.

Her dad nodded. "That penny helped me get rid of the jitters," he said. "I think it helped me play better, too."

"Where's the penny now?" Marcus asked.

"It's in my memory box," their dad said. "I'll go get it." Then he walked out of the room.

Mia inspected her new charm. "Hey look, it has my name on it," she told Marcus.

He squinted until he saw Mia's name

engraved in tiny letters on the charm.

"Here it is," their dad said, coming back into the room. He pulled a tarnished penny from the wooden box he was holding.

"This looks ancient," Marcus said.

"It was made the year I was born," their dad said, pointing to a number on the penny.

Mr. Robinson had a faraway look on his face as he looked at the penny. "I had a sweet jump shot in high school," he said. "And I still have skills."

Mia and Marcus giggled.

Mr. Robinson looked at the twins. "You two up for shooting hoops in the driveway to warm-up before practice?"

"I'm there already," Marcus said, rushing out of the room.

"Race you," Mia said, whizzing past her brother. She could hardly wait to get outside. Shooting baskets with Marcus was nothing new. She helped him warm up before all of his games. But this was the first time her dad had invited her to join the two of them. That was something that Marcus and her dad always did by themselves.

Mia glanced back at her dad just before she opened the front door. "Don't forget to rub your lucky penny," she teased.

• • •

Later that afternoon, Mia walked through the doors of the gym ready for her first practice. Only a few other kids were there.

Looking around quickly, Mia spotted Gabbie sitting at the end of the first bleacher.

"You beat us here," Mia said, plopping down beside her. Two more girls were sitting on the other side of Gabbie. Mia leaned over and waved at them.

They smiled and waved back.

"What's up, Gab?" Marcus said as he passed by. He headed to the other end of the long bleacher where the boys were seated.

Just then, Coach Dilbert jogged across the

court. "Welcome to the new Titans co-ed team!" she said, stopping in front of the kids. "I'm Coach Dilbert."

"Where is Coach Rakestraw?" Marcus asked, wondering about his old Titans coach.

"He's coaching one of the older boys' teams this year," Coach Dilbert said, looking at the boys. "I know you guys will miss him. But I think you'll have fun on this new team, too."

"I'm glad you all made it to the first practice," the coach continued. "We'll practice every Monday and Wednesday at six o'clock. And we have one game a week—on Thursday or Saturday. Our first game is this Saturday against the Wolverines."

"They are one of the toughest teams in the league," Marcus whispered to Juan.

Everybody counted off. Then the coach lined them up in pairs. Mia was paired with Rupert.

Oh, no! Mia thought. Rupert was in her fifth grade class, and he was impossible to get along with at school. He was always bullying the other kids.

"It's just my luck to get paired with a *girl*," Rupert groaned.

"Let's start with warm-up laps," Coach Dilbert said. "Take two laps around the gym, passing the ball back and forth with your partner."

Mia and Rupert completed the first lap without saying a word.

Rupert broke the silence during their second lap. "You're not getting *tired* yet are you?" he teased as he tossed Mia the ball.

"No," Mia said, catching the ball.

"Is this your first time passing a basketball?" Rupert asked.

Mia rolled her eyes and giggled. "Of course not!" she said. "I shoot hoops at home with Marcus all the time."

"Well, you better practice all you can," Rupert said. "You have to be *really* good to be a Titan."

CHAPTER

3

"This is the last round," Marcus said, bouncing the ball toward Mia.

It was less than an hour before the Titans' first game, and the twins were finishing up their pregame practice in the driveway.

Mia grabbed the ball and stepped behind the white line Marcus had drawn on the pavement with a piece of chalk. It was the same distance from the goal as the free-throw lines on real basketball courts.

Mia hunched over and began her free-throw ritual. She bounced the ball once to the right, once to the left, and one time in the middle. Then she took her shot and

watched as the ball rolled into the basket.

"Good shot," Marcus told his sister.

"Thanks," she said. "I hope I can do that in today's game."

· · ·

"Good luck!" the twins' parents said as they took their seats in the bleachers. Their mom tapped them on the head with her blue-and-white pompom.

"Thanks!" the twins said, heading for the Titans' bench.

Mia slid her duffel bag under the bench and sat down. Then she unzipped her jacket and slipped out of it. She was anxious to show off her new Titans jersey.

"Calling all Titans!" Coach Dilbert shouted.

Mia took a deep breath as she bent down to pull up her gym socks. "Oh, no!" she muttered. She was still wearing her charm bracelet. And it was against the rules for players to wear jewelry during games.

"Calling all Titans!" Coach Dilbert repeated.

"Come on, Mia," Marcus said as he rushed past her to the team huddle.

Mia unhooked her bracelet and stuffed it in a pocket on the side of her duffel bag. But the basketball charm peeped out. She looked at it and suddenly remembered her dad's lucky penny.

"Come on!" Gabbie pleaded. "They're waiting on us."

Mia quickly rubbed the charm between her fingers and poked it deep into the pocket. "I'm coming," she said.

Marcus scored the first basket of the game. It was a turn-around jumper in the paint.

"Go-ooo, Marcus!" Mia shouted from the sideline.

The Wolverines answered with two points.

"Swoosh!" Gabbie screamed when Juan delivered the Titans' next basket.

Late in the game, Coach Dilbert called out,

"Gabbie and Rupert, you two are in!"

Rupert scrambled off the bench for the second time and hustled back on the court.

Mia nudged Gabbie. "Give it your best shot," she told her friend. Mia parked herself back on the edge of the bench anxiously waiting for her turn to play.

Rupert scored a fast two points. Then he fired off another shot. It was a horrible miss.

"AIRRR BALLL!" the Wolverines fans shouted.

Rupert's forehead wrinkled and his eyes bulged.

The Wolverines grabbed the ball and scored an easy basket that trimmed the Titans' lead to one point.

"Timeout!" Coach Dilbert yelled, making a *T* sign with her hands.

The players on the court jogged toward the sideline and began to huddle together in a tight circle.

Rupert stormed past his teammates and headed for an empty chair at the end of the

Titans' bench. He swung his leg and gave the chair a mighty kick.

"Uh-oh!" Mia and her teammates whispered.

Coach Dilbert marched over to Rupert. "Pick it up!" she said, pointing at the chair.

Rupert placed the chair back on its four legs and crossed his arms.

"Now sit down, Rupert!" Coach Dilbert snapped, tapping the back of the chair. "You're benched for the rest of the game!"

Rupert sank down in the chair as Coach Dilbert rushed back to the Titans' huddle.

"Mia," the coach said, looking over at her. "We need you. Are you ready to play?"

Mia jumped up, excited. "Yes," she said.

"You're in," the coach yelled, pushing Mia toward the court.

Marcus passed the ball to Mia right away. She was posted just under the basket. She caught the ball and threw it in the air like it was a brick. The ball swept past the goal, missing it by at least two feet.

"Take your time, Mia! Take your time!"
Coach Dilbert yelled from the sideline.

The Wolverines popped in another quick
basket and took the lead.

With only fifteen seconds left, Juan snatched
the rebound and dribbled down the court.

"Over here!" Mia shouted.

Juan hurled the ball toward her.

Mia spun toward the basket and bounced
off her feet. She released the ball in midair.
It jiggled around the rim of the basket and
dropped in as the game clock buzzed.

The final score flashed on the scoreboard.
Titans 38. Wolverines 37.

"Yeah!" Mia's teammates screamed, jump-
ing up and down and congratulating her.

Mia pumped her fist in the air and did a
little victory dance.

Marcus just sighed as he met their teammates at center court to shake hands with the
Wolverines.

CHAPTER 4

Mia slowed to a stop as she finished her last warm-up lap at Monday's practice. But Rupert kept running.

"Hey, that was the last one," she yelled.

"The coach is making me run extra laps," Rupert yelled back.

Just then, Coach Dilbert blew her whistle and assigned everyone their new practice partners. "Mia, you and Rachel are together."

"*Yesss!*" Mia screamed to herself. She was glad to be paired with anyone except Rupert. But her excitement didn't last long.

Rachel had to leave practice early. And Rupert didn't have a partner yet.

"You two can pair up for the rest of today's practice," the coach said to Mia and Rupert.

Mia sighed as she and Rupert ran down the court.

"Why did you have to run extra laps?" Mia whispered as they waited for the passing drill to start.

"Because of the chair I kicked at our game," he said.

"Let's go, team!" Coach Dilbert said, starting the drill.

Mia and Rupert sprinted down the court passing the ball back and forth.

"Take a breather!" Coach Dilbert yelled when everyone finished the drill.

Mia rested the ball on her hip. "Why did you kick that chair anyway?" she asked Rupert.

He dropped his head. "Because I was mad," he said. "I missed a really big basket."

"Maybe you should try counting," Mia suggested.

Rupert gave her a strange look. "Counting?"

he asked. "What are you talking about?"

"When I feel myself getting angry, I count to ten," Mia said.

Rupert gave her a strange look. "You do?"

"Yep," Mia said. "It helps me calm down."

"Hmmm," Rupert said. "I've never tried that."

"Maybe you should," Mia said.

Coach Dilbert blew her whistle. "Same drill in the other direction!" she shouted.

"By the way," Rupert told Mia when the drill was over, "that was an awesome basket you scored in our game."

Mia was surprised. "Um, thanks," she said. That was the first time she had ever heard Rupert say anything nice to anyone.

• • •

The Titans' second game was against the Jaguars on the other side of town.

"Welcome to Jaguar Country!" Mia said, reading a banner above the scoreboard when she walked into the gym. Mia and Marcus passed the Jaguars' sideline as they headed to the visitors' bench.

"Who is *that*?" Mia asked Marcus. She pointed to Number 8 on the Jaguars' team. He was the tallest boy on their team.

"That's Skyscraper Scottie—don't you remember him from last year?"

Mia shook her head no.

"He's one of the best players in the league," Marcus told his sister.

When they reached the Titans' sideline, Mia rubbed her lucky charm and tucked her bracelet in her duffel bag. Then she joined the team huddle.

The game was off to a quiet start until Marcus stole the ball from a Jaguar and scored a one-handed sinker. Then the game started to move more quickly, with both teams scoring several baskets each. But Mia thought things were about to explode when Rupert got slapped with his third foul.

Rupert stomped off the court angrily.

"Don't forget to count!" Mia pleaded as Rupert walked past. She held her breath as he slid into a chair. One by one, Rupert's fingers popped out as he silently counted to ten.

"Whew!" Mia whispered.

"Mia, you're in!" Coach Dilbert shouted.

"Okay," Mia said. She was glad she rubbed her lucky charm before the game.

Mia made a free-throw and bumped up the Titans' lead by one point. But her most amazing play in the game came when she blocked a shot attempt by Skyscraper Scottie.

It all happened when he lunged in the air to shoot the ball. Mia was standing smack dab in front of him. But she got a head start and sprang off her feet before he did. When Skyscraper Scottie let go of the ball, Mia's hands smashed it down.

"Whoa!" the Titans yelled. They danced around on their feet, swapping high fives.

Titans fans in the stands went wild. They had also cheered for Marcus. He scored a

whopping ten points in the second half.

Marcus's teammates congratulated him as soon as the game was over. "Good game, Marcus!" they said.

He flashed a winning smile. But before he could say thanks, his teammates disappeared.

They were talking to Mia.

"Hey, Mia, wait up. You've got to tell us how you blocked Skyscraper Scottie's shot," one of the Titans yelled.

"Yeah, that was some play," Natalie said.

Marcus quietly walked behind them.

"Scottie's shots hardly ever get blocked," Juan said.

Mia didn't say a word. She just smiled. Then she reached into the pocket of her duffel bag and pulled out her charm bracelet.

Marcus's eyes widened as he watched Mia snap the bracelet back on her wrist. "Hmmm," he muttered under his breath. "Maybe that charm really *is* lucky."

CHAPTER

5

It had been more than a week since Mia rubbed her charm for good luck on the basketball court. That was how long it had been since the Titans' last game. The team's third game was canceled because not enough players showed up from the other team. But Mia had found another place to test out her lucky charm—at school.

Mia had just sat down at her desk in Ms. Jordan's classroom. She was digging in her backpack for her pencil. As Mia pulled her arm out, her charm bracelet rattled. Mia closed her eyes and rubbed her basketball charm.

"What are you doing?" Marcus whispered, turning around.

Mia's eyes flashed open. "Rubbing my charm," she whispered back. "For good luck on my presentation."

Marcus studied his sister's face. "So, you *really* think it helps, huh?" he asked.

Mia opened her mouth to speak, but Ms. Jordan interrupted before Mia could answer.

"Good morning, class," she said. "Let's settle down and get our day started."

Mia smiled. This was her favorite day of the school week. On Wednesdays, everyone in the class had to bring in a writing assignment to read aloud. Mia couldn't wait to share hers.

"Who wants to go first?" Ms. Jordan asked after she called the roll.

Mia and three of her classmates raised their hands.

Ms. Jordan picked Mia to go third.

When it was her turn, Mia hurried to the

front of the room. She held *Mia's World* in front of her with both hands. Then she read the headline. "Rainbow Recreation Center Starts First Co-Ed Basketball Team in League."

She paused before she read the article. "This year, the girls got a chance to join a girls' basketball team. Then they almost didn't get to play. But thanks to a new co-ed basketball team, everyone gets to play."

The class grew quiet.

"It is a fun experience to play on a team with boys and girls," Mia read aloud. "Everyone can learn from each other."

Mia read about the great plays that Carmen Rodriguez, Rachel Moore, and her other female teammates made for the Titans. "The girls helped the basketball team win their first two games," Mia read. When she said that, all of the girls in the class cheered.

"Shhh!" Ms. Jordan scolded through a smile.

Gabbie's hand flew up as soon as Mia finished the article.

"Yes, Gabbie," Ms. Jordan said.

"Mia scored the winning basket in our first game!" she told her teacher.

Ms. Jordan smiled. "Really?" she asked. "Mia, do you want to tell us about it?"

Mia blushed. "It was nothing much," she said. "Just a lucky shot."

Marcus tapped his foot.

"Well that was a fantastic article!" Ms. Jordan said. "Good luck with the rest of the basketball season."

When she got home from school, Mia tried to study for her spelling test. But every time Mia looked at her word list, she started daydreaming about scoring another winning basket.

Her mind had drifted miles away when the doorbell rang.

Mia's mom opened the front door.

"Come in, Gabbie," Mia heard her mom say. "Mia is upstairs. Why don't you go up and get her for practice."

A few seconds later, Gabbie strolled into Mia's room. She had come over to ride to practice with the twins. "Hey, you're not dressed yet," she said.

"I know," Mia said. "I've been trying to study for Friday's spelling test, but I didn't get much done. Now I'm thinking about skipping today's practice."

"But you have to go," Gabbie said.

"But I don't know my spelling words."

"You can study tomorrow," Gabbie said.

Mia closed her notebook. "I guess you're right," she said. "I'm sure my charm will bring me luck for the test anyway."

• • •

Marcus did everything right at practice that afternoon.

"Way to go, Marcus," Coach Dilbert kept repeating.

Mia heard her name a lot, too. But it was for different reasons.

"Wake up, Mia!" the coach snapped when she was daydreaming and didn't realize it was her turn to shoot.

"Hustle, Mia," Coach Dilbert yelled when Mia should have moved quicker.

"Hurry back!" the coach shouted when Mia asked if she could go to the restroom. By the time Mia returned, she had missed the dribbling drill.

But Mia didn't really mind. With her lucky charm, Mia was beginning to think she didn't need to work so hard at basketball anymore.

CHAPTER 6

The twins ran errands with their mom the next day after school. The minute they got home, Mia hurried to her room and pulled out her spelling list. This was the first time the Titans had a game on a school night, so Mia wanted to study before they left.

"Alibi," she said, reciting the first word on the list. Mia closed her eyes and played with the charms on her bracelet as she spelled the word.

Suddenly, Mia's eyes popped open. She flipped her wrist back and forth inspecting her charms. "It's gone!" she shouted. "It's gone!"

Marcus dashed into her room. "What's

wrong?" he asked. "Did you lose something?"

"My lucky charm. It's gone!" Mia cried.

"Are you sure?" Marcus asked.

"Yes. It's not here," she said. "See?" Mia stuck her wrist in his face.

"Maybe it just fell off," Marcus said calmly.

Mia dropped to her knees and frantically wiped the carpet with her hands. "Please check the stairs!" she told Marcus.

He rushed out of Mia's room.

By the time he came back, Mia was sprawled out on the floor searching for the charm. He stepped over her and sat on the edge of her bed. "I didn't see it," he said.

"What am I going to do?" Mia asked.

Marcus shrugged his shoulders. "I don't know," he said.

"I need it for tonight's game," Mia moaned.

That evening, Mia arrived at the basketball game wearing a black baseball cap snugged low on her head.

"What's wrong?" Gabbie asked.

"I lost it," Mia said, telling Gabbie about her charm.

"I'm sure you'll still have a good game," Gabbie told Mia.

Mia wasn't so sure. She slipped the baseball cap off her head and slid to the end of the bench. She hoped Coach Dilbert would forget she was there. But she didn't.

Just before halftime, the coach yelled her name. "Mia, you're in," she said.

Mia rose, paralyzed with fear.

"Go for it, Mia!" Gabbie said.

Mia jogged onto the court.

Juan threw her the ball right away. Mia reached for it, but it slipped through her hands. After that, everything went downhill. Mia double-dribbled twice and missed an easy layup. Then, after she tripped over her own feet, a short boy on the other team stole the ball from her and scored two points.

"I knew I shouldn't have played on a team with a bunch of girls," Rupert whined when

Mia finally returned to the sideline.

Mia glared at him. She wanted to remind him of the baskets he had missed and the time he got benched. But she didn't.

"Just ignore him!" Gabbie whispered.

Marcus made up for Mia's mistakes. He played one of his best games ever. He had a record ten rebounds and raked up sixteen points. He also had three assists.

"Good game!" Mia whispered to Marcus when the game ended. Then she grabbed her stuff and darted to the closest exit.

The other Titans hung around and showered Marcus with compliments.

"Super game," one of his teammates said.

"Yeah, you saved the game," Juan said.

Mia's parents were waiting outside the door.

"I played horribly, just horribly!" Mia said.

"Oh, it wasn't that bad," her dad told her.

Her mom gently squeezed her shoulder. "Everyone has an off game every now and then," she said.

Marcus shoved the door open.

His parents smiled at him.

"You had a great game, son," his dad said. "We're proud of both of you."

Marcus took a bow. "The kid is back!" he announced. "Did you hear them cheering?!"

His parents nodded softly.

Mia gave him a faint smile.

As soon as they got home from a dinner out, Marcus dashed into the kitchen and grabbed the carton of ice cream from the freezer.

Mia leaned against the dishwasher and slid to the floor. She kicked off her sneakers.

"One scoop or two?" Marcus asked Mia.

"Make mine a double," their dad said, sitting down at the table.

"I don't want any," Mia mumbled.

"But you picked the flavor this time," Marcus reminded her. They had begged their mom to stop by the ice cream shop earlier that afternoon. She agreed to buy a quart of ice cream if they saved it until after dinner.

"Oh, come join us," Mia's dad told her.

"No thanks," she said.

Mia climbed the stairs and moped all the way to her room. Then she sat down at her desk and opened her notebook.

A minute later, Mrs. Robinson stuck her head through the doorway. "Honey, it's not like you to pass on ice cream. Is tonight's game still bothering you?" she asked.

Mia sighed. "I just wish I hadn't lost my charm," she said. "And I need to finish studying for tomorrow's spelling test."

"Hopefully we'll find the charm," her mom said. "Right now just focus on your spelling words. Do you need some help?"

"No, I'll be fine," Mia told her mom.

Mia stared at her spelling words. She tried to concentrate, but she kept reflecting on the mistakes she made in the game. And she couldn't get the lucky charm off her mind.

CHAPTER

7

Mia struggled through her spelling test that Friday morning.

Ms. Jordan passed them back at the end of the day. The teacher frowned and placed Mia's test facedown on her desk.

Mia was scared to turn it over. Slowly, she lifted the corner of the paper and peeked at the other side. A big "70" glared at her.

It was worse than she had imagined. She had never scored below an 80 in her entire life.

Mia folded the paper in half and stashed it in her backpack before anyone could see it.

Gabbie rushed up to Mia when the bell rang. "I got a ninety," she said. "How did you do?"

"Not good," Mia said. "I can't seem to do anything right since I lost my lucky charm."

When Mia got home she searched her room again. She found a dirty gym sock, thirty-seven cents, a stick of gum, and a candy wrapper. But she didn't find the charm.

THUMP! THUMP!

Mia heard a familiar sound below her window. She peeped out. Mr. Robinson had come home early, and was shooting hoops with Marcus.

Mia watched them for a while, then she headed outside.

Marcus smiled when he saw her. "Want to play?" he asked.

"No," Mia said. She went to the corner of the garage and took her bike helmet off the shelf. She strapped it around her head. Then she pushed her bike out into the driveway.

"Where are you going?" Marcus asked.

"For a ride," Mia said.

"Don't forget we have a big game coming

up next weekend," Marcus said. "You know you should practice."

Mia frowned. She knew she couldn't play basketball as well as Marcus could, but she didn't think he needed to rub it in.

"I don't need to practice anymore," Mia announced. "I'm quitting the team."

Marcus's and Mr. Robinson's heads jerked toward Mia. They looked at her as if she were a ghost.

Her father's voice was calm. "You want to quit the basketball team?" he asked.

"Yes," Mia said. "Without the charm, there's just no use."

"You can't mean that," her father said.

"Are you serious?" Marcus asked. "I didn't know the charm meant *that* much to you."

Mia looked at him. He sounded like he really cared.

Just then, the front door opened. "Marcus, telephone. It's Juan," their mom interrupted.

"Coming," Marcus said.

With a dazed look on her face, Mia stared at Marcus as he ran in the house.

Mr. Robinson walked to the garage and wheeled out his bike. "Mind if I join you for that ride?" he asked his daughter.

"I don't mind," Mia said.

They rode down the sidewalk in silence.

Mr. Robinson pedaled to Mia's side. He glanced over at her and chuckled. "Seeing you on your bike reminds me of when you first learned how to ride."

"It does?" Mia asked.

"It sure does," he said. "When you got your first bike, your mom and I would give you a push to get you started. But every time we let go, you would fall over in the grass. Then you would pout and say you hated that bike."

Mia giggled. "I don't remember saying that."

"Well, you did," he said. "But you would go back the next day and try to ride it again. Finally, you learned to balance yourself."

Mia smiled. "I remember that," she said. "I

rode all the way down the street."

They coasted down a shallow hill.

"And look at you now. You're riding a twelve-speed," her dad said. "I'm glad you didn't give up on riding that first bike."

"Me, too," Mia said. She took her hands off the handlebars. "Look, no hands!"

"Mia, you know basketball can work the same way, if you don't give up," her dad said. "Once you start believing in yourself again and not that charm, you'll be just fine."

Gabbie was pushing her bike up the Robinsons' driveway when Mia and her dad got home from their ride. She had come over to watch a movie with Mia.

The girls parked their bikes by the garage and went inside. They grabbed some snacks from the kitchen and rushed to the family room just in time to watch the movie. When it ended, Mia clicked off the TV.

"Do you want to spend the night after our game next weekend?" Gabbie asked Mia.

Mia gazed down at the carpet. "Um, I'm not playing in that game," Mia said softly.

Gabbie shot Mia a surprised look. "You're not?" she asked.

Mia shook her head. "I'm not playing in any more games," she said. "I'm quitting the team."

Gabbie stood up. "You can't quit the team," she said in an airy voice. "We promised we'd play together. Best friends' honor, remember?"

Mia sighed. "I know," she said. "But without my charm, I'm just horrible. You saw how terribly I played at our last game. I don't want to let our team down like that anymore." Mia looked at her friend, hoping she would understand.

Gabbie whirled around in a huff and turned her back to Mia. "I've got to go home!" she said. She stormed to the front door.

Mia followed behind her. "Do you still want me to spend the night next weekend?"

"I don't know," Gabbie said. She closed the door as she left.

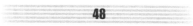

CHAPTER

8

After breakfast the next morning, Mia went to the hall closet and pulled out an old, decorated shoe box. It was stuffed with pictures, magazine cutouts, and ideas for *Mia's World*.

Mia carried the box to the kitchen table and took the lid off. She thought working on her newspaper would be a perfect way to help her forget about the charm.

Suddenly, Marcus sneaked up behind her and slid a sheet of paper on the table. "Will this help?" he asked.

Mia read the top of the page. "LOST: GOLD LUCKY CHARM." She gave Marcus a curious glance.

He grinned. "Keep reading," he pleaded.

"Have you seen a gold basketball charm? If found, please call 555-1212." Mia smiled. That was their phone number.

Mia read aloud. "Reward: three Jason Carter trading cards."

Mia gawked. "Your Jason Carter trading cards?" she asked.

"Yeah. They were the only thing I could think of . . . besides my new Jason Carter jersey," he said. "And I *really* want to keep that."

She couldn't believe Marcus was willing to give the trading cards away.

"Why are you being so nice to me?" Mia asked, giving Marcus a suspicious look.

Marcus shrugged. "You looked so miserable when you lost your charm," he said.

Marcus gazed down at the table. "And it's kind of fun playing basketball with you."

Mia smiled and picked up the flyer. "This is a brilliant idea!" she said. "Maybe Mom can help us put them up."

Later that afternoon, Mrs. Robinson drove the twins all over town. First, they stopped at the places that they visited the day Mia lost her charm—the library, the grocery store, and the ice cream shop. No one at those places had seen the charm. But they did let Marcus and Mia post their flyers. On the way home, they also taped flyers up to telephone poles, at gas stations, and at their school.

"Maybe it will turn up after all," Mia said as they pulled in their driveway.

The Robinsons ate dinner as soon as they got home. Turkey tacos were Mia's favorite. She usually ate them in a hurry. But this time she was the last one to finish. She was dreading what she had to do after dinner.

Mia's mom looked at her as she crunched the last bite of her taco. "Are you sure about your decision?" she asked her daughter.

Mia dropped her head. "Yes," she mumbled.

Mrs. Robinson pulled the Titans telephone roster off the refrigerator and dialed Coach

Dilbert's phone number. "Hi, Coach Dilbert," she said, speaking into the phone. "This is Mia Robinson's mom."

Mia's heart fluttered.

"I'm fine, thanks," Mrs. Robinson said. "Mia has something to tell you. Hold on, please."

Mrs. Robinson gave the phone to Mia.

She took a deep breath. "Hi, Coach Dilbert," Mia said softly. "Um, I wanted to tell you that I . . . uh . . . I've decided not to play basketball anymore. I'm quitting the team."

"Mia—this is quite a shock," Coach Dilbert said. "But why?"

"I . . . I just don't want to play anymore," Mia told her. She didn't want to tell her coach the real reason she was quitting the team.

"Are you sure, Mia?" Coach Dilbert said.

"Yes," Mia squeaked.

"Well, if you change your mind, let me know," the coach told her.

"Okay," Mia said.

The next week dragged by. No shooting hoops in the driveway with Marcus, no basketball practice, and not a single visit from Gabbie.

Mia still felt terrible about breaking her promise to her best friend. That had bothered her all week. And something else was bothering her, too. The Titans' next game was just around the corner. Mia couldn't decide if she should attend the game. By Friday, she was leaning toward not going.

"What time is tomorrow's game?" the twins' dad asked that night at the dinner table.

"Four o'clock," Marcus said.

Mia twirled a spaghetti noodle around her fork. "Do I *have* to go?" she asked.

"Mia, we *always* go to the basketball games," her mom said, sipping her iced tea. "Why wouldn't you go this time?"

Mia sighed. "Because I'll feel like an odd-ball," she said. "And everyone will want to know why I quit the team."

Mia shoved her fork in her mouth.

"You don't have to go this time," her dad said. "But it would be great for you to support Marcus and the team."

Mia spun another noodle onto her fork.

"Give it some more thought," her mom said. "If you don't go, Dad or I will have to miss the game, too. You can't stay home by yourself."

"I know," Mia said softly. She knew how much her parents loved watching their basketball games. She hated to be the reason one of them might have to miss Marcus's game.

By the next morning, Mia made her decision about attending the basketball game. And she made up her mind about something else. She decided it was time to visit Gabbie.

Mia pressed the doorbell twice.

Gabbie cracked the door open and peeped out. "Oh, hi," she told Mia.

"Good morning," Mia said. "May I come in?"

Gabbie opened the door. She was still in her pajamas. "You're here awful early."

"I just came over to apologize," Mia said. "I'm really sorry about breaking my promise."

Gabbie smiled a faint smile. "I'm okay about you quitting the team," she said. "I mean I want you to play, but I guess I'll be all right without you. I'm actually having fun."

Gabbie tugged at the bottom of her pajama top. "Are you coming to the game today?" she asked.

"No," Mia said. "I'm not going."

"Well, you can still sleep over tonight, if you want to," Gabbie said.

"Thanks! I can't wait!" Mia said.

CHAPTER

9

Mia watched their dad's car back out of the driveway. It was strange seeing Marcus and her dad leave without her and her mom. Mia felt like a family tradition had been broken, and it was her fault.

Mia dragged herself to the couch and plopped down. She picked up the TV's remote control and surfed the channels. Nothing was on that she wanted to watch. *What do I do now?* she asked herself.

Mia headed up to her room and packed her overnight bag. Then she finished reading the new mystery book her mom gave her.

Mia peeked out her bedroom window.

They're still not back, she told herself, thinking about Marcus and her dad.

Suddenly, Mia did something she had never done on a Saturday. She studied. Mia was working on the fifth word on her spelling list when she heard the car pull into the driveway.

Mia jumped off her bed and dashed downstairs. "How was the game?" she asked as Marcus and their dad walked in the house.

Juan was right behind them. Mia had forgotten that he was spending the night with Marcus. "I mean how was the game?" she asked again, trying not to sound so interested.

Marcus shook his head. "It was ugly! Just plain ugly," he said.

"You mean we lost?" Mia asked.

"*We* lost," Marcus said. "You're not on the team anymore, remember?"

Mia sighed. "Well, what happened?" she asked, following them into the kitchen.

"The other team played better than we

did," Marcus said. "And I fouled out!" He reached into the refrigerator and pulled out two sports drinks.

"I had a rough game," Juan said, taking a bottle from Marcus.

"Was the score close?" Mia asked.

"They beat us by two lousy points," Juan said, shaking his head. "Can you believe we lost by *one* basket?!"

Mia remembered the winning basket she scored in the Titans' first game. A startling thought crossed her mind. *Maybe I could have scored a basket in this game, too.*

"We might have won if Rupert didn't get benched again," Marcus said. "We really needed him in the second half."

"He got benched *again?*" Mia asked. "Did he kick another chair?"

"No," Juan said. "He got mad because we were losing. So he refused to join our huddle at halftime."

Mia buried her face in her hands. "He

was supposed to count to ten!" she muttered under her breath. She wondered if he would have kept his cool if she had been there to help remind him to count.

The phone rang as the boys walked out of the kitchen.

"Hello," Mia said.

"Hi, did they tell you about the game?" Gabbie asked.

"Yeah," Mia said. "I can't believe the Titans lost."

"And it was so close," Gabbie said. "Did they tell you about the three points I scored?"

"No!" Mia said. "That's great." Those were Gabbie's first points of the season. Mia was impressed with how hard her friend kept working at basketball. *Even harder than I did,* Mia thought to herself.

"When are you coming over?" Gabbie asked.

"In a few minutes," Mia said.

"See you soon," Gabbie told her.

Mia went to get her overnight duffel bag,

which was sitting near the front door.

"Mom, I'm ready," Mia called up the stairs. She walked to the window in the family room and peeked out. It was almost dark, but Marcus and Juan were shooting hoops in the driveway. Marcus made four baskets in a row.

As Mia kept watching, she thought about all the times she played basketball with Marcus in that very same driveway. She made lots of baskets back then. And she was doing that long before she had a lucky charm.

CHAPTER

10

It was 5:30 on Monday afternoon. The Titans' next practice started in thirty minutes.

Mia rummaged through the top drawer of her dresser. She found her WNBA T-shirt, slipped it over her head, and grabbed her duffel bag.

Then Mia crept down the stairs.

"Wait for me," she yelled to Marcus.

He was walking out the front door. "Where are you going?" he asked, turning around.

Mia smiled. "With you," she said.

Marcus raised his eyebrows. "To *practice*?" he asked.

Mia nodded her head.

Marcus's forehead wrinkled. "But I thought you quit—"

"I changed my mind," she interrupted. That past weekend, Mia decided that she wanted to get back on the basketball team. She had told her parents and Gabbie, but she wanted to surprise Marcus.

Marcus shook his head and chuckled. "Have you told Coach Dilbert?"

"No, not yet," Mia said as they walked out to the van.

Their dad drove them to practice. He usually just dropped them off. But this time he parked the car. "I'll stick around until you talk to the coach," he told Mia.

"Let's go," Marcus said, hopping out.

Mia took a deep breath before she entered the gym. She wasn't sure what to expect from her old teammates. After all, she hadn't seen most of them since her embarrassing performance at her last game.

Mia's eyes locked straight ahead as she

walked toward the players' bench. It looked like it was at least a mile away. She was surprised that no one paid her any attention—no one except Gabbie.

Her best friend ran toward her. "You're really back!" Gabbie said.

"I hope so," Mia said, sitting down.

Rupert approached her. "What are you doing here?" he asked in a loud voice.

"I'm back on the team," Mia said softly. "If Coach Dilbert lets me play again."

"I missed you at the last game," Rupert said, gazing down at the court.

Mia's mouth flopped open. "You did?"

"Yeah," he said, lowering his voice. "I forgot to count."

"Line up, Titans!" Coach Dilbert yelled. She walked over to Mia. "Hi there. Are you here to practice or to watch?"

"Um, well, I'd like to get back on the team," Mia said.

Coach Dilbert studied her face. "Are you

sure this time?" she asked in a firm voice.

"Yes," Mia said, looking her in the eyes.

The coach smiled. "It's very brave of you to come back," she said. "You've missed a lot. But if you hustle, you can make a great contribution to the rest of the season."

"I won't let the Titans down," Mia said.

"Hop in line for the shooting drill," Coach Dilbert said.

"Thanks," Mia said. Then she took off running. She was halfway across the gym when the coach blew her whistle.

"Mia!" Coach Dilbert yelled.

The floor squeaked as Mia stumbled to a stop. She glanced back at her coach. "See me after practice," the coach said sternly.

"Okay, coach," Mia said. Her dad walked in the gym as she turned back around. Mia smiled and waved at him.

The first few drills were hard for Mia. She had only missed a week of practice, but she felt totally out of shape. When practice

ended, Mia chugged nearly a gallon of water. Then she hurried over to Coach Dilbert.

"Mia," the coach said, sounding serious. "You'll have to make up for the practices you missed."

"Okay," Mia said softly. She hoped she didn't have to run extra laps like Rupert did when he got benched.

"I want you to pick up the basketballs and stack them back on the racks after our practices this week," the coach said.

Mia glanced at dozens of balls scattered across the gym floor. "Okay," Mia said.

Then the coach pointed to a giant dust mop propped in the corner of the gym. "After you put up the balls, you can use that duster to sweep the court."

Mia's eyes widened.

"I've already checked with your dad," the coach added. "He'll wait for you."

Mia squatted, scooped up two basketballs, and carried them to an empty rack.

"See you later, BALL GIRL!" a few Titans shouted at Mia as they left the gym.

• • •

It was a rough week for Mia, but she was still glad to be back on the team. She felt that way until the day of their next game. On Saturday afternoon, she was dressed in her Titans uniform and ready for her pregame warm-up with Marcus. But as she bent over to tie her shoelaces, her charm bracelet jiggled. She looked at it and thought about her lucky charm. Suddenly, she felt unsure of herself.

Just then, Marcus walked into her room. "Are you ready, sis?" he asked.

"I guess," Mia said. She sighed as she headed outside.

Mia and Marcus took turns shooting baskets. Mia missed her first few warm-up shots. But she kept trying until she found her rhythm. Her courage started to come back after she made two baskets in a row.

Mr. Robinson stuck his head out the front door. "It's almost time to leave for the game."

"Okay," the twins said.

Marcus tossed the ball to Mia. "I'm thirsty," he said. "I'm getting a bottle of water."

"Bring me one, too," Mia yelled as Marcus scampered in the house.

The phone rang the second Marcus walked in the kitchen. "Hello," he said, answering it on the first ring.

"Yes, hello. I'm Mr. Gordon calling from Gordon's Ice Cream Shop," the voice on the other end of the line said. "I'm calling about a missing lucky charm."

Marcus's eyes sparkled. "A gold basketball charm?" he asked.

"Yes, we found it," Mr. Gordon said. "It had rolled under a wastebasket."

"My sister is going to be sooooo happy," Marcus said. "Thanks for calling."

"Daaaad!" Marcus yelled, hanging up the phone. "Guess what?" he said with a smile.

Mr. Robinson trotted down the stairs. "What is it, son?"

"That was the owner of the ice cream shop," Marcus said. "He found Mia's charm!"

"That's great news," Mr. Robinson said. "But we can't go pick it up now. We'll be late for the game."

Marcus's dad leaned close to him. "Let's not tell Mia about the charm right now," he whispered. "We'll surprise her after the game."

Marcus smiled a sneaky smile and slid his fingers across his lips. "My lips are zipped," he whispered.

Marcus grabbed the bottled waters from the refrigerator and turned to go back outside. "Oh!" he said, freezing like a statue.

"What's wrong?" his dad asked.

Marcus sighed. "I guess I better go get the reward." He dragged up the steps and headed to his room.

CHAPTER

11

At the start of the game, Mia's nerves got the best of her. She was wide open when Gabbie tossed her the ball. But instead of taking a shot, Mia passed it like a hot potato.

"The ball won't burn you," Coach Dilbert told her after that play. "Next time you're open, shoot the ball."

Mia sat out for a breather, but she was called back in the game after Rupert committed his second foul.

The referee blew his whistle loudly to restart the game.

Mia was fouled by another player almost immediately.

The referee's whistle blared again. "Blue team, Number Nine, two shots at the free-throw line!" he yelled.

Mia stepped to the free-throw line. She bounced the ball once to the right, once to the left, and once in the middle.

Her teammates clapped and tried to encourage her. "Come on, Mia!"

"MISS IT!" the opponent's fans shouted.

Mia missed her first shot.

Marcus stepped over to her and squeezed her shoulder. "Concentrate, Mia!"

"MISS IT! MISS IT!" she heard again before she took her second shot.

Mia dribbled two more times. Finally, she released the ball. It sailed through the hoop.

Marcus threw his fist in the air and spun it around. "Way to go, sis!" he shouted.

Mia lifted her head like a peacock and darted down the court, smiling and ready for the next play.

• • •

The Robinsons piled into their minivan.

Mia pulled her charm bracelet out of her duffel bag and hooked it back on her wrist.

"We need a victory celebration," the twins' dad said. "How about some ice cream?"

"I want mudslide triple fudge," Marcus said.

Mia smiled to herself. She couldn't believe her parents were breaking their "no dessert before dinner" rule. But she wasn't going to remind them about it. "I'm getting a double scoop of wild strawberry scream," she said.

• • •

"Are you Mr. Gordon?" Marcus whispered to the bald man standing behind the ice cream shop counter.

"Every day," the man said with a smile.

Marcus smiled back and leaned toward him. "I'm Marcus Robinson," he said. "I talked to you earlier today about my sister's charm."

"Oh, yes," the man said in a low voice. "I'll go get it. It's in the safe."

"Where's your sister?" Mr. Gordon whispered to Marcus when he came back.

Marcus pointed to Mia. "Over there," he said.

Another shop worker dipped Mia's ice cream and passed her waffle cone across the counter. "Here you go," he said.

Mr. Gordon looked at Mia. "I think this belongs to you, too," he said. He stretched his arm across the counter and opened his hand.

"My charm!" Mia gasped. She covered her mouth. "How did you know?"

Mr. Gordon picked up the flyer that was lying next to the cash register. "As soon as I found it, I called the phone number," he said.

Mia grinned. "The flyers were my brother's idea," she said.

Marcus dug into his back pocket and pulled out his three trading cards. He slowly slid them across the counter. "Here's the reward," he said.

Mr. Gordon picked up the cards and inspected them. "Jason Carter, huh?" he asked.

Marcus nodded.

"I bet you've been collecting these for a long time," the man said.

"Yes," Marcus said.

Mr. Gordon studied the cards again. "Why don't you just hold on to these," he said. He passed them back to Marcus.

Marcus's eyes brightened. He gave Mr. Gordon a crooked smile. "Okay," he said. "Thanks. Thanks a lot!"

"Mr. Gordon, we appreciate your calling us about the charm," their dad said as he paid the bill. "Mia is very happy to have it back."

As soon as Marcus sat down at the table, Mia raised her ice cream cone in the air like she was making a toast. "Here's to my MVB," she said, looking at her brother.

"Your what?" Marcus asked.

"My MVB. Most Valuable Brother," she said. "Thanks to you, we found my charm."

"I'm your only brother," Marcus told her.

They all laughed.

"Hey, you haven't put your charm back on your bracelet," Marcus said.

Mia looked at her charm. "There's no rush," she said calmly.

"But I thought you couldn't wait to get it back," Mia's mom said.

Mia bit her cone. "I couldn't," she said. "I still really like it. But . . . "

"But what?" Marcus asked.

"I'm just not sure if I *need* it anymore," Mia said. "I play pretty well—when I practice."

"But what about the winning basket you scored in our first game?" Marcus asked.

"That's not the only basket I've ever made," Mia said.

Marcus licked his ice cream. "But what about that big block against Skyscraper Scottie?" he asked.

"I think I just jumped in the air first."

Mia leaned back in her chair. "I got a hundred on my spelling test on Friday . . . without my lucky charm," she announced. "I just had to study the words."

Her parents smiled.

Marcus licked his ice cream again. "I think *you* are your own lucky charm," he told Mia.

"Maybe you're right," Mia said. She picked up the charm and rubbed it between her fingers. "But I think this is still a *little* lucky."

Everyone gave Mia a surprised look. "It *is*?" they asked.

"Yeah," she said. "It got us dessert before dinner."

She giggled and slurped the bottom of her cone.